PALM BEACH COUNTY
LIBRARY SYSTEM
3650 Summit Boulevard
West Palm Beach, FL 33406-4198

Dear Parents:

Congratulations! Your child is taking
the first steps on an exciting journey.
The destination? Independent reading!

STEP INTO READING® will help your child get there. The program offers
five steps to reading success. Each step includes fun stories and colorful
art or photographs. In addition to original fiction and books with favorite
characters, there are Step into Reading Non-Fiction Readers, Phonics Readers
and Boxed Sets, Sticker Readers, and Comic Readers—a complete literacy
program with something to interest every child.

Learning to Read, Step by Step!

Ready to Read   Preschool–Kindergarten
• big type and easy words • rhyme and rhythm • picture clues
For children who know the alphabet and are eager to
begin reading.

Reading with Help   Preschool–Grade 1
• basic vocabulary • short sentences • simple stories
For children who recognize familiar words and sound out
new words with help.

Reading on Your Own   Grades 1–3
• engaging characters • easy-to-follow plots • popular topics
For children who are ready to read on their own.

Reading Paragraphs   Grades 2–3
• challenging vocabulary • short paragraphs • exciting stories
For newly independent readers who read simple sentences
with confidence.

Ready for Chapters   Grades 2–4
• chapters • longer paragraphs • full-color art
For children who want to take the plunge into chapter books
but still like colorful pictures.

STEP INTO READING® is designed to give every child a successful
reading experience. The grade levels are only guides; children will progress
through the steps at their own speed, developing confidence in their reading.
The F&P Text Level on the back cover serves as another tool to help you
choose the right book for your child.

Remember, a lifetime love of reading starts with a single step!

For my Little League grandsons Jacob, Yoni,
Andrew, and Aaron —D.A.A.

For Enoch —S.R.

Text copyright © 2016 by David Adler
Cover art and interior illustrations copyright © 2016 by Sam Ricks

Visit us on the Web!
StepIntoReading.com
rhcbooks.com

Educators and librarians, for a variety of teaching tools, visit us at
RHTeachersLibrarians.com

Library of Congress Cataloging-in-Publication Data is available upon request.
ISBN 978-0-593-43236-5 (trade) — 978-0-593-43237-2 (lib. bdg.)

Printed in the United States of America
10 9 8 7 6 5 4 3 2 1

This book has been officially leveled by using the F&P Text Level Gradient™ Leveling System.

GET A HIT, MO!

by David A. Adler

illustrated by Sam Ricks

Random House New York

"Bam!" Mo Jackson says.

He swings a carrot stick.

"Bam!" he says again.

"It is a home run."

Bam! Bam! Bam!

"Finish your snack,"

Mo's father tells him.

"It is almost time to go."

Mo swings the carrot stick

one more time.

Then he eats it.

Mo's parents take him
to the baseball field.
Mo's team is the Lions.
Today the Lions are
playing the Bears.

Mo is smaller than the others
on his team.

He is younger, too.

Coach Marie tells the team
when each player will bat.
She tells them where to play
in the field.

Mo will bat last.
I always bat last,
Mo thinks.

He will play right field.

I always play right field, Mo thinks.

No balls ever come to right field.

"Play ball!" the umpire calls.

Mo stands in right field.

He watches the Bears

score two runs.

The Lions are up.

Mo sits on the bench.

He watches his team bat.

He also watches the pitcher.

Whoosh!

Whoosh!

That pitcher throws fast,

Mo thinks.

How will I get a hit?

The Lions don't score.

Mo's team is losing, 2–0.

It is the end of the second inning.

It is Mo's turn to bat.

Whoosh!

"Strike one," the umpire calls.

"Mo! Mo!" Coach Marie shouts.

"Stand close to the plate."

Mo stands close to the plate.

Whoosh!

"Strike two."

"Mo! Mo!" Coach Marie shouts.

"Swing the bat."

Whoosh!

Mo swings the bat.

He swings too late.

"Strike three," the umpire calls.

"You are out."

Mo stands in right field.

He watches the other

team's batters.

When the ball is too high or too low,

they don't swing.

When the ball is just right,

they swing and hit the ball.

That's what I'll do, Mo thinks.

In the fourth inning
it's Mo's turn to bat again.
When the ball is just right,
Mo swings.

But he swings too late.

Mo strikes out again.

I want to hit a home run,

Mo thinks.

But all I do is strike out.

It is the last inning.

There are two outs.

Mo may be the last batter
of the game.

People are cheering.

Coach Marie is shouting.

Mo can't hear Coach Marie.

Whoosh!

"Strike one,"

the umpire calls.

The cheering gets louder.

Coach Marie shouts louder.

Mo still can't hear her.

Whoosh!

"Strike two."

One more strike and
the game is over.
People are standing.
People are cheering.

Mo turns to hear what
Coach Marie is shouting.
When he turns,
his bat turns, too.

Crack!

The ball hits Mo's bat.

The ball rolls quickly past
the pitcher.
"Run! Run!" Coach Marie
and other Lions shout.

Mo runs.
He gets to first base.

The ball keeps rolling.

"Run! Run!"

Mo keeps running.

He runs to second base.

The two Lions who were

on base score.

"We win! We win!" Coach Marie
and others shout.

The Lions run to Mo.

Mo's parents run, too.

"This time, I didn't strike out," Mo says.

Coach Marie says, "This time you won the game."